About those Dragons…

by Jane Ellen Holliday Wilson

Illustrated by Glenda Mace Kotchish

ISBN-10: 0998971510
ISBN-13: 978-0-9989715-1-3

Library of Congress Control Number: 2018901868
Room For Writing Press, Richmond, VI

Dedication:

Dedicated with love and gratitude…

…to our sacred circle of powerful writing women, and to writing people (adults and children) everywhere…

Janie and Glenda

...and to my grandchildren, Wilson and Kelsey, who loved this book the first time I read it to them…

Glenda

…and to Lindsay and Natalie and Elias and Wilson, my precious story-time buddies…

Janie

Dragons are
Everywhere in life

Sleeping under
The house

Waiting to be
Awakened

Already awake
And storming about

We may as well
Learn to
Befriend them

Again a Specter stands at my door

A formidable foe,
A dragon flinging
Burning,
Scorching flames.

She's not the first dragon.

She's just the current dragon.

They are so tiresome
With their attention catching
Flames!

It's so hard to see
The lesson she brings,
When it is surrounded in
All those flames.

The battle is not won
By attempting to slay her;
I have the scorch marks
And the scars to prove that.

The only way to get this done
Is to look deep into
Her eyes,
Calming the flames that make
Her
Burn so uncomfortably.

Then, reach into her mouth
And pull forth
The jewel that is
Lodged therein.

Careful now,
She is a dragon after all.

This is what she's come for.
If you will only take it,
She will go away.

And this way there are
No burn marks and scars,
No scorched earth either.

No burning bridges
Left to haunt you,

And all your
Progeny.*

*Ask a grown up to explain what this word means.

Just the jewel.
It's there.
Fix your eyes
On hers
And reach for it.

The Beginning

www.roomforwritingpress.com

About the Author

Jane Ellen Holliday Wilson (Janie) has led a full life, and continues to do so; an early career in interior space planning and design; two beautiful daughters off doing interesting things with their lives; a second career in the social sector; and a second family that includes four more delightful young grown-ups, two grandsons (so far) who love this book already, and, of course, a fabulous husband.

In the midst of all this, Janie began writing fiction, poetry and so forth—this very book started as a poem. In 2017 she published, with her illustrator Glenda Kotchish, an anthology of poetry, memoir and short story entitled *Make No Assumptions*. Prior to that she published *Room For Poetry* along with her sacred circle of powerful writing women. It was in that sacred circle that her current dragon was first hatched.

The Illustrator

Glenda Mace Kotchish is a painter, ceramic artist and writer. She is the owner of an art center in Richmond, Virginia where she helps people share their artwork with the world. She and Janie are long-time friends and collaborate in weekly writing sessions.

www.ingramcontent.com/pod-product-compliance
Lightning Source LLC
Chambersburg PA
CBHW042209170626
46815CB00012B/100